Sleepy Possum Teacakes

by Hoss Wildfire ©

AuthorHouse™
1663 Liberty Drive
Bloomington, IN 47403
www.authorhouse.com
Phone: 833-262-8899

This book is printed on acid-free paper.

ISBN: 978-1-6655-2417-9 (sc)
978-1- 6655-2418-6 (e)

Library of Congress Control Number: 2021908460

Print information available on the last page.

Published by AuthorHouse 10/21/2021

authorHOUSE

Sleepy Possum Teacakes

"Pssst...pssst...Sleepy! Wake up!...wake up!" a voice was heard coming from under the front door of Sleepy Possum's tree trunk. Charlie Cricket was a very nervous cricket. For being such a small creature he sure could get everyone all fired up. Sleepy finally opened the door and yawned widely and with sleepy eyes still trying to adjust to the light, he whispered "What is it my good man that you must come waking me up at this hour?"

"Sleepy! Sleepy! You must come to the edge of the forest!" shrieked the little six-legged insect "Oh, all right, all right..." yawned Sleepy Possum. " I will be ready in just a moment. "Care for some teacake, my friend?"

"abso...lutely not!" said the cricket. Sleepy Possum's custom was to always have a bite of teacake before he embarked on an adventure...whether it was serious or trivial. Charlie Cricket seemed to always be having a crisis of some sort. Sleepy Possum of course always knew better that most times it was just something that the little cricket made into a big deal.

"Well now, my good man, what is all the commotion about?," inquired the all knowing marsupial.

"See here old chap, there seems to be a fly in the ointment," replied Charlie Cricket. " What does that mean?" asked Sleepy as he yawned again.

"Yes, yes indeed...someone's planning to get married, Sleepy and that isn't good," replied the little creature.

"Um...allow me a moment" he munched on some tea cake "so...someone getting married and that isn't good? Now why is that not good and why does concern us my friend?" asked the opossum.

"Sleepy you don't understand, if she marries him we'll all be without a home! gasped Charlie. "Without a home?, preposterous, my good man...the forest is safe from harm...it's been home to all for many centuries" replied Sleepy.

Charlie looked really distressed about the whole affair and so Sleepy finally set before him a saucer with a piece of tea cake and some fresh tea "Have some old friend?"

"No, thank you," replied Charlie. "This is not a social call...this...is serious, Sleepy...very serious!"

"Alright then please elaborate on the matter," he motioned toward the tea cake and then said "if you won't then I will" and he sat down at the table while the cricket stared in disbelief. "Well get it off your chest Charles if you will,"

With that Charlie's left eyebrow raised and the look of his disapproval of being called Charles was clearly evident. "You see if lady Rachel marries that man he will sure flatten the forest and thus destroy our homes Sleepy," he straightened his antenna and wiped his brow and then he took a deep breath.

"My, my, Charles, seems we might indeed have a problem. I will see into it myself. In the meantime why don't you find yourself a niche somewhere here and take a good nap?"

So Sleepy Possum went out into the forest and yelled out to Oliver Owl, "Oliver, Oliver can you please show yourself?" Within seconds a sound of fluttering wings was heard and then, "Who, Who, I say calls upon this old owl at this time of night?" asked Oliver Owl.

"Sorry I beg your forgiveness my wise old friend it is I, your old friend, Sleepy looking at a problem that might be something of concern",

Whooo, whooo, well in that case let's have it then and let us examine the facts," replied Oliver.

Oliver's immense size dwarfed the opossum's by a large margin and if those two weren't friends, it could surely present a problem making it most likely that Oliver would be the victor in a battle. But Sleepy wasn't here for confrontations… he was here to implore the old owl for his due diligence in the matter that Charlie had now set before them. And with that Sleepy went on to explain the concerns of Charlie Cricket.

Sleepy then had Charlie, who by now had hopped to his side, second his explanation with his testimony and the owl intently heard it all. This news was a genuine concern if there was a possibility that they would lose their home. It would affect every inhabitant of the forest.

"So, what plan have you devised, old friend?" asked the owl.

"I propose that we investigate this fully and get all the answers immediately." said Sleepy. He then pulled a kerchief from his coat and produced some teacakes. "Care for any my friend?"

"Don't mind if I do!" and the great old owl swooped down and had a helping of delicious tea cake. All of a sudden the owl's eyes grew heavy and he became sleepy. "Old friend, seems your tea cakes are so good and filling and now I am sleepy...what do you wish me to do about our new problem?"

"When you're out on a flight would you go swoop close to Miss Rachel's window and see if you can hear anything that may validate Charles's concern? "Done!...but first I must go sleep off this intoxicating mix of flour and other good things and upon awakening I will go and eavesdrop on Miss Rachel and see what I can find out. I bid thee a good night" and with that he flew off into the darkness.

The sun's rays peered through the tree branches and life began stirring in the forest. There was a lot of commotion and once again there was a knock at Sleepy's door. "My, my," yawned Sleepy...so much for sleeping in late...oh well this calls for some more teacake and I will see who's at my door." It was Rascal Raccoon.

"Sorry Sleepy sir! ...I am here to report for Oliver Owl Sir!"

"Yes, yes...I gathered as such" with an annoyed look on his face."Very well, then let's have it...what is the status of said situation?"

"Sir...it appears that Miss Rachel is indeed readying herself for a wedding. Oliver swooped by her window and as he did so he saw a very beautiful dress hanging on her wall," replied Rascal Raccoon.

Sleepy held up his right hand with a motion for the raccoon to lower his voice as he was known for talking loudly and asked " So, the lady has finally been discovered by a lord? Well how quaint? It was bound to happen at some time or another. Beautiful, pure of heart women do not need to live out their lives alone," he said.

There was a tiny sound behind them and it was Charlie Cricket chirping a little song. Now Charlie was the nervous type but he always made up a little song to calm himself. With every word he would rub one wing across the other...it was indeed quite soothing.

There was a look of calmness on his face...which was quite rare and that implored Sleepy to ask why he was so happy. "Charles? Charles? Are you well my friend? Nice melody my good man but please...would you mind sharing as to why your mood is so different from last night?"

The cricket played one last note on his wing and breathed " I, Sleepy, am in looooooooove, " He had this dreamy look on his face.

Both Sleepy and Rascal stared at one another in disbelief. Charlie was in love? How could this have occured? And with all he revealed last night, no one could have guessed. How soon!

"Well then Charles," testing the small creature. "So I take it there is to be two weddings then?"

"No, no I just need one wedding...just one," he sighed

"Seems our fellow forest resident is deeply in love Sir!" mused Rascal.

"That my dear friend seems to be the case," Sleepy cleared his throat. "what is the news on Miss Rachel in detail please"

"Well Sir, word from Marian Mouse verifies the news that it seems there is this young chap named Sir William who has paid many visits to Miss Rachel. They have been going out at least once a week. She invited him in one day for tea and teacakes and since then he's been a regular visitor , Sir"

"Very Well then," said Sleepy with a look of interest " what are we to make of this fellow? Is he worthy of our young Miss Rachel?"

"Sir this man comes from royalty...He is to be heir to our lord King Edward's throne. He is the best man for the job from what I gather, Sir," said Rascal.

Sleepy took a bite of a teacake as he thought to himself "Hmm, clearly this would mean that if Miss Rachel was indeed to marry this young suitor, everything would change. The residents of the forest might indeed lose their home." But he knew that Miss Rachel loved the woods and he comforted himself with the thought that she would not wish to leave her little "piece of heaven". So, in short things might get complicated should the young man take the throne and have her take a place next to him.

"Very well then, Rascal would you alert the entire forest residents that we are to have a meeting in front of Miss Rachel's house before dusk today?" said Sleepy.

"Yes Sir, right away Sir," and with that, Rascal Raccoon made his way back to alert the others. "and as for you my good man?" Sleepy turned to Charlie Cricket clearly still in "another world"

"What say You? old chap, is this time the last time you fall for someone? You remember your last so called "love of a lifetime?" For sure that time we all thought you were under some type of spell!" smiled the opossum.

"Uh ah....well yes well it's different this time," said the little cricket.

Sleepy had that look an opossum gets when he knows all too well that something isn't quite what it appears to be.

"Very well then," said Sleepy "if you wish not to discuss the matter then we won't" and with that he proceeded to walk toward his tree trunk in hopes that he had one last teacake left somewhere in a hidden spot. "Wait! Waaaaaaaiiit!" yelled the little cricket.

"Yes?...yeeeeeeees?" Sleepy paused in order to let the little cricket catch up to him. "What dost thou have to say oh great winged musician Romeo of the forest?"

"Well...you see it's like this...uh...um...I didn't think I would fall so soon" sighed Charlie.

"Let's have it my good man! I am an old opossum and there isn't much time here before I have a hunger attack."

"Well, You see Sleepy, we crickets get very excited when we go on a journey in the forest...and" "And?" replied Sleepy as his stomach led out a loud rumble.

"I saw this beautiful fairy in the forest by the birdbath Miss Rachel has for the birds" he sighed

"She is so beautiful!"

At that moment Sleepy got a smirk on his face and had to look away. Clearly the cricket was in love although he had no clue that what he fell in love with was nothing more than a fairy figurine as Sleepy had seen Charlie's new "love" just recently.

"Charles, May I ask You a question?" Sleepy looked at the cricket with questioning eyes. "Yes, of course! What is your question, Sleepy?" Charlie said with his right antenna now up with intrigue.

"My good man...how much of a conversationalist is this fairy?" inquired Sleepy. "uh um, convo who?" inquired Charlie

"Yes Charles...meaning someone who is good at talking and listening" said Sleepy.

"Well she don't ever talk...never heard her say a single word as a matter of fact. But she has a nice smile and those eyes! Oh my gosh! Those eyes!"

"Charles? Charles!" interrupted Sleepy. (ahem) Sleepy cleared his throat " This fairy is she always in the same spot always?"

"Yeeeeees," replied Charlie with glazed eyes. "She's always in the same spot waaaiiiiting!"

"All right my good man let's go meet this special lady." with that Sleepy headed toward the forest. And then the little cricket chirped excitedly and began hopping by Sleepy's side. It wouldn't be long before they arrived and there she was. Only this time there was water pouring from her mouth down towards a basin below her. Charlie got pale and almost fainted. "What is it Charles...are you feeling well?" asked Sleepy with a smirk on his face.

"Well I,uh, um, er didn't know she could do that!" exclaimed Charlie.

"Well then Charles, let us examine the facts...she is always in the same spot, in the same pose, doesn't utter a word or sing and now she's got water coming out of her mouth...hmmm Why of course yes!...my good man I'd say she is a Fountain Fairy! Made of the finest materials to provide water for the birds of the forest. Yes Charles I'd say you are right...she is a beauty alright...but she isn't alive at all... is she Charles?" Poor Charlie was looking a bit pale, if it can be said that a dark cricket's color can be compared to a lighter shade of pale.

"Sir! Sir!" the residents of the forest are ready for the meeting!" came a voice from a distance. It was Rascal Raccoon. There was a line of forest creatures behind him. When the last creature arrived it was then that Sleepy made his way through them to the front of the house.

"Excellent…Very well then, places, places everyone, " said Sleepy as he found a spot just in front of the doorstep. Like an experienced director on a movie set he raised his right paw, he commanded, "Let us alert Miss Rachel that we have come to pay her a visit" And as if it was all rehearsed, from the smallest creature to the biggest, all of them began to make noise. It was not long when the door opened and Miss Rachel came out in the company of Sir William to meet them. Just then Sleepy made his way to the front of the crowd and turned to face Miss Rachel and Sir William. Miss Rachel was wearing a smile and so was Sir William, "I'd say my dear that we are graced with some very good company are we not?" With that Miss Rachel went and stood right in front of them, her skin radiant, her eyes with a gleam and and her golden hair catching the last rays of the sun for the day. All the creatures stared in disbelief at her beauty. She asked, "and to whom do I deserve the honor of this grand visit?"

And with that Sleepy raised his his right paw in acknowledgement of the question that was posed and he spoke, "It is merely the humble residents of the forest gathering to pay you a visit madam"

"Yes, yes William and I have taken notice, and what is the nature of this visitation?" asked Miss Rachel. "We have concerns, madam, as you know we have been your neighbors for many, many years and now we are faced with what could be a great dilemma. We are worried about our home." replied Sleepy with that look of concern that could be noticed by everyone present.

"I see very well and what is the concern that has all of you in front of my house all at one time?" She eyed all of them with very enchanting eyes as she took Sir William's hand in hers.

"Well...we have seen that you what appears to be a suitor and we feel that it could change things for us." said Sleepy with a rather questioning tone in his voice.

Miss Rachel spoke, "Fear not, for whatever future is in store for myself with this wonderful man in my life, the forest will remain as it is and has been for decades, untouched and should I decide to take Sir William's hand by his side on his throne, his royal army will be at your service to keep it that way." she then gave Sir William a look that made him speak. "Friends, indeed to my dearest Miss Rachel, I have promised all the comforts that a woman of her beauty and grace deserves. It is my intent that she never lack for anything much less peace of mind" It was then that Sleepy turned around and addressed the creatures and with a look of confidence said "Well then, there You have it, we can all go home and rest comfortably that all will remain the same...and as for you Charles," everyone looked around at Charlie Cricket, " let us never assume that just because something new occurs within our midst...that it indicates a worst case scenario!" Charlie gulped and became pale once again as all eyes were on him then the crowd burst out in laughter and everyone made their way back home. Sleepy then turned around and said to Miss Rachel and Sir William. "My Lord and Lady, we are grateful that we have such honorable neighbors in our presence. I bid thee a good evening and a good night"

"Wise old friend, we are also grateful to you for being such a good mentor and friend to all the residents of the forest. Good night old friend" replied Miss Rachel and with that she and Sir William went back inside the house.

"Uh, um, what happens now?" asked Charlie.

Just then a loud rumble came from within Sleepy's empty stomach, I don't know about you my good man, but I believe I've got one teacake left at my cottage...care to join me old friend?"

With that Charlie dropped the leaf he had been munching on and said "absolutely Sleepy!" And they went back into the forest as the sun set in the west as it had for many many sunsets before that.